BY THE SAME AUTHOR

Some Postwar English Novelists

The Short Stories of Sean O'Faolain: A Study in Descriptive Techniques

Short Stories

Goodnight, Morning

Poetry

Seasons & Remembrance

Beginnings, Endings

Past Present

Against the Stream
(with Aquarelles by Gerhard Elsner)

Late Motley

MOMENTS IN TIME

Jo Rippier

for
Susan & Stephen Ware,
a small expression of
thanks for such
a warm welcome in
your beautiful home,

26 July 2009

COLIN SMYTHE LIMITED

This volume first published in Great Britain in 2004
by Colin Smythe Limited, Gerrards Cross, Buckinghamshire SL9 8XA

British Library Cataloguing-in-Publication Data

A catalogue record for this book
is available from the British Library

ISBN 0-86140-454.8

Produced in Great Britain by Biddles Ltd, King's Lynn, Norfolk

Contents

Palm Dove

Lost stranger from
        a distant land
alone its call
        unaccustomed
cadence impinging
        on the ear
each day at
        dawn and dusk
a signal sent
        but not received.

On looking down
        what will it see
a summer landscape
        not like its own
suffused with sounds
        but not its own

its bubbling lament
        rising just before it falls.

Sporting Notes

6 November 1955: 1 mallard, 3 teal. Pool by the river. One very good shot.

"One very good shot." How transparently false those four words of self-praise sound after an interval of half a century. At the time I'm sure I was not aware of this. But how could I have been? Youth is a period of constant self-delusion. I can still see that unfortunate bird – impacted for ever on my mind – even after such a long passage of years. It rose from the pool, had reached a point at which it was almost safe. A very long shot. The bird stopped in mid-air as if arrested by some invisible hand, dropped like a stone. It was indeed a wonderful shot.

A "wonderful" shot. How is it possible that I could slip back into the exaggerated terms of youth? Perhaps one never ever really grows up. Random images, sounds, or references can switch one back to an incident in the distant past, somehow always on instant recall. I have never kept a diary, but I did have a little book in which I recorded what I had killed, at a time when shooting was still a passion. Even now, as I leaf through this slim volume, each entry brings back a moment when some poor creature was sacrificed to my love of the chase. And even if I have long since lost any real urge to shoot, since such instincts ease with time, I still remember the thrill – yes, thrill – when I was successful. I suppose, although this is an unfair comparison, it is a similar sensation to what a bullfighter feels when he goes in over the horns to make a kill. With one significant difference. In the case of the person behind the gun, there is no danger.

Nevertheless that short entry brought back other memories. Memories with which those few words had no connection. Yet there was a connection. The scene was suddenly reproduced again in the theatre of my mind. I had left the house, crossed the road, gone through the gate. I once again registered the mood of that moment as I went down the hill across darkening meadows in the direction of the pool whose waters reflected darkly in the gathering dusk.

And I can still remember the very second when I first saw her. A young girl caught in white light, and etched, held for ever in my mind's eye. A dance at a friend's house. She was standing by herself, seemingly taking no part in what was going on around her. Not aloof, but somehow separated from her surroundings. When I addressed her she looked up, not even appearing to be aware of my presence. When she did, she blushed. She was very shy. As indeed we both were.

How innocent such occasions then were. She was almost eighteen. I was several years older. I had just finished military service in the Far East from which I had returned, a little wiser in the ways of men but still very untried in the ways of the world. Where I had been stationed, the possibilities of meeting young women with whom I might have gone out just did not exist. There were of course the bars, and other places. Since one of my responsibilities had been the recording of statistics on various sexually transmitted diseases, I had been quickly cured of any inclination I might have had to experiment in such places.

"Would you like to dance?" I asked.
She nodded.

And so on down the slippery slope. The light was going fast, my boots squelched in the muddy ground as I took the approach to the pool which made it possible for me to remain unseen. I slowed down, walked more carefully. I could still make out ripples, grey oily ripples on the surface of the water, but no dark shapes.

This was in some ways an unlikely spot to be waiting for wildfowl, birds which are notoriously shy. But I had discovered that they did come in at dusk, when they could expect to remain undisturbed. From where I stood I could look out into a darkening foreground. Far ahead, and way beyond and above the river, was the rising glow of city lights. And yet, as darkness deepened all around me, an increasing sense of being totally alone, isolated in this small space.

Suddenly I heard what I had been waiting for. The sounds of duck approaching. They flew in and splashed down into the water. Something must have disturbed them, as they rose again almost immediately and flew towards me. I was fortunately placed. By the time they had become aware of me, it was too late. Two with one barrel – the birds were in close formation – and a third with the second. Satisfactory, very satisfactory, I remember thinking. Coldly, rather than in jubilation. The shots echoed, seemed unnaturally loud.

Even at university, where I had started immediately after being released from the army, I still had to find my feet. There was a continuing sense of isolation. There were only two women's colleges, and thousands of male students.

We danced. At first a little awkwardly. I talked, as she seemed unwilling to say very much. I fear I may have gone on at inordinate length, as shy people sometimes do once they get going. She didn't seem to mind. The evening passed on wings. At the end, when I asked her, she appeared keen to meet again. And on this occasion the roles were reversed. She spoke. Freely. I cannot now recollect exactly what she spoke about. She was serious, almost earnest. But everything she said had my full attention. It was all new. Exciting. Full of promise. I was only home for the weekend. I asked if I could write to her. She seemed pleased with this suggestion. I did write.

Probably because of the lights in the distance my own surroundings took on a much darker appearance. I waited on, listening attentively. One advantage of having the glow of the city in the distance meant that even on really dark nights one had the possibility of making out the silhouettes of birds passing against the light.

I did write. I wrote several letters in the course of the following weeks but received no reply.

And then a letter arrived. It was short and to the point. I can still see, in my mind's eye, certain sentences. "We seem to have little in common. I must concentrate on my studies. . . It was nice meeting you, but I don't think we should continue seeing each other."

I was on the point of leaving. A single duck flew in at some distance from me. Like the others, this bird took off again shortly after landing on the water. This time it did not fly in my direction. It was indeed a long shot. But it went home.

As I now recollect I realise it was the day on which I had received the letter. I have the distinct impression that I was even thinking about it when I pressed the trigger. Which is of course why I experienced rather strange feelings when re-reading that short entry in my game book:

6 November 1955: 1 mallard, 3 teal. Pool by the river. One very good shot.

A Simple Question

"What are those birds, Daddy?"
"They're curlews."
"Why are they flying like that?" the small boy asked, as he stared up into the sky. Birds were diving and wheeling above their heads.

"They're worried," the man said.
"Why, Daddy?"
"Well, they have their nests here. And we may be disturbing them."
"Could we find a nest?"
"I don't know," said the man, "but we could try."

They had driven out into the country on a bright spring day. Now they were walking, quite by themselves, through marshy fields just below hills which rose in front of them. The turf under their feet was soft, springy. The two of them quartered the ground where they were. The man told the small boy to look and step carefully. They walked up and down, up and down, for at least half an hour. The small boy remained in a state of excitement and anticipation. For a while they even went separately before finishing up standing opposite each other.

"Well, I did warn you," the man said, "nature does its best to help these birds."

The small boy stared intensely at his father following his every word. Then he looked down. There was perhaps a yard between them.

And there, in that small space, was an open nest. In it were four large olive mottled eggs, with the thinner ends pointing inwards.

The father suddenly realised how concentratedly the boy was staring, before he too noticed the nest. They remained standing where they were, quite motionless.

The boy looked, and looked. He could not have put it into words, but he had a sudden sense that he would live for ever.

Martial Arts

It has to be admitted – if only in retrospect – that there is a certain rather curious pleasure to be derived from polishing boots. Particularly if this has to be done intensely, over a period of weeks. As the original pimples – no doubt specifically designed for some useful purpose – are either ironed away or polished into insignificance, one slowly develops an unusual intimacy with one's footwear. A relationship distinct, personal, and lasting. Something one never forgets.

Of course it is not the boots which are responsible for this. They are merely a tangible manifestation of that extraordinary state one enters the moment one leaves civilian life.

It could have been another planet. For those first few weeks one is cut off from the rest of the world, forced into the company of complete strangers with whom one has to live together on the most intimate of terms.

Including total exposure to the arbitrary moods of another group of men whose sole aim it seems to be of making life as unnatural and unpleasant as possible. Those responsible for basic training.

There is a retreat into self – perhaps facilitated

via the boots – in the attempt to adapt to alien circumstances. Everything is different, seemingly designed for discomfort, all of it contributing to a psychological de-stabilisation. All sense of what is personal, familiar, disappears – seemingly for ever – from the moment of entry into barracks.

What's more, the presence of rats under the beds at night then just becomes an almost natural part of new, unfamiliar, distinctly hostile surroundings. Even such officially sanctioned tasks as painting coal white, or cutting the grass with scissors are suddenly not strange, but merely part of a totally new normality.

Yet none of this was in essence unexpected. There had even been preparation in the form of army camps organised from school. Perhaps because one was surrounded by those one knew, the whole exercise merely emphasized and expanded an impression of the world viewed from the comforting vantage point of the familiar. Even night exercises were hardly intimidating in that one was not alone. Any danger was imagined, or implied. It had no substance in reality.

I was vaguely surprised that others in my squad seemed – at least outwardly – so unshaken by their new surroundings. Some, coming from a boarding-school background, were obviously used to living their private lives, so to speak, in public. What the others thought I shall never know as, apart from banter, little that was personal was ever revealed in those first weeks.

One instinctively sought anonymity. In that respect a uniform was a definite advantage since once dressed, apart from differences in height and shape, we all looked exactly alike. An amorphous mass of clumsy khaki.

Managed, drilled, chased from early morning to exhaustion at night. Constant harassment, directed by flinty NCOs who knew exactly what they were doing and why they were doing it. There was even a very occasional lifting of pressure when some unfortunate recruit was publicly abused. Always a sense of relief that it had happened to someone else, as this mass of men was broken down into units which slowly began to move in a military manner.

The professionals all seemed so sure, so confident. One could not imagine them hesitating at a moment of crisis. An inner discipline had been instilled. Their training would have stood them in good stead. At least that was how I then thought. If I now look at old photographs I can again see what I then must have unconsciously resisted. The necessity to become an unthinking automaton.

Photographs are always revealing. Certain features come through more strongly than others. As the images fade with time, one may notice details which might not have registered initially. Any photograph is, unlike a picture, immutable. It is a part and reflection of its time. An oil painting, for example, is so much more. It will not normally fade, but will reflect different things to each generation.

The soldiers on these old photos seem, even now, to exude a clarity of line and expression. They are formed, hard, unshakable, qualities which I no doubt secretly admired, but which I found impossible to assimilate or adopt. Which may well have affected any progress I had hoped to make.

There was something about the eyes which reminded me of a mad bull. Not that I had ever seen a mad bull, but I should have been warned.

"So you want to become an officer."
"Yes, sir."

I think it was at that point I noticed a slight swelling on the man's right cheek.

"Now, I've been looking through your papers.

You say here," he continued, stabbing a finger at the form in front of him, "that you wish to serve with your present unit before joining the Royal Artillery. Why?"

"Well, sir, I wanted to be relatively near home for the first three months while I was doing basic training." I paused.

"Yes?" More of a hiss than a question. Again I should have caught on.

"I thought I'd then have a chance of going abroad. Later." I added somewhat lamely. I fear, inadvertently, almost repeating the words on the poster 'Join the army and see the world'.

The hand holding the form had begun to quiver slightly. The spot on the cheek became – like the rest of the man's face – livid. I waited.

"Do you really think that the army is there just for your convenience?"

"Well, sir, since I'll only be serving for a couple of years, I did actually feel . . ." my voice faded as I looked across the table. At this point I think even I began to appreciate that the interview was not going well.

The man's hand went to his swollen cheek. I

realised that he was suffering, and not only from the inadequacy of my answers. He scribbled something on the paper in front of him, and almost immediately dismissed me. It was a remarkably short interview, leaving little doubt in my mind as to how I had performed.

There must have been a number of reasons why I never became an officer, none of which had anything to do with the interviewer's toothache. Yet, before I started military service, everything had seemed so simple. If I had not exactly sailed through school, I had never been confronted with anything which brought me close to elementary realities.

My mind filled with illusions of grandeur distilled from what I had read at the time, I saw myself leading troops . . . regiments. Divisions! Or going off on dangerous missions ahead of a small band of chosen soldiers into the jungle, or straight up cliffs. Even the steepest of cliffs presented little challenge to my over-heated mind.

"Right!" barked the staff-sergeant, "You!" pointing at me "will get these five men across that ditch and over that five-bar gate. In precisely 25 seconds. You are under enemy fire. Go!"

I looked at the five men, all of them out to do

well. Preferably at my expense. They were all clearly officer material. Why I was so sure, I no longer know.

I now also have no precise recollection of what went wrong. Somehow my leadership qualities, in which up to that very moment I had had supreme faith, like my voice in the interview, faded. I seem to remember that the others got through before me, something on which the staff-sergeant commented ferociously. After that it was downhill all the way.

The Art of the Short Story

“Right. Prep for tomorrow. You are all going to write a story. Did I hear anything?” Groans round the class.

“I am even going to make things easy for you. I will give you three words, and you will build a story around them. Do I make myself clear? The three words are: ‘man’, ‘woman’ and ‘dog’.”

For some strange reason I completely forgot all about this until I was reminded by a classmate the following morning as we went into school. In something of a panic I pulled out a sheet of paper and, after brief reflection, wrote the following:

“I’m leaving,” said the man.
“Good,” said the woman, “and you can take the dog with you.”

As far as I remember, I was given a mark of five out of ten. There were a few words scribbled underneath: “This was very clever, which is why I have given you five marks. Unfortunately though, it’s only a beginning. The bare bones, so to speak. But slightly better than not having written anything. Do I make myself clear?”

I think we both got the message.

Hatches, Matches and Despatches

I happened to be staying in the town where I had gone to school, a time still very clearly registered in my memories of early life. At breakfast I glanced through the local paper. After a certain age one's attention tends automatically to be drawn to some sections more particularly than others. For example the deaths column. I will freely admit that what I note first – after the name – is whether the person who has died was younger than myself. If that should be the case, for rather morbid reasons, the day picks up. This does not reflect well on character, but pretending that one does not have such thoughts would be equally reprehensible.

The names meant nothing to me. Which was hardly surprising. But then my attention was caught by one name which all of a sudden seemed familiar. John Mount. I looked again. John Mount. One year younger than myself. For once this discovery gave me no sense of comfort. The name, together with the age, could hardly be a coincidence.

I sat there, quite still, my eyes resting on that short entry in the local paper, thinking. Thinking back. John Mount. We had been friends, very close friends. We had even been in the same class all the way through school. We had similar interests. Both at school, and for a period afterwards, we had been almost inseparable. Relatively soon after leaving school I moved away, while John stayed in his home town, where he made a career. We remained in touch for several years.

I stopped. Something was wrong with the way my thoughts were being formulated. What was it? I suddenly realised. It was the word "we". In fact I had kept in touch. For a considerable period of time. I had been very happy to do so. We always found it easy to talk to each other. John always seemed delighted to hear from me. He would tell me what he was doing, even occasionally asked me about myself.

Then, at some stage or other, I decided to stop calling, and wait for him to contact me. He never did. So, although there was no clear cause for it, a break in communication occurred. We never spoke to each other again. And now we never would.

I put the paper down, but remained sitting where I was. As I continued to think back, a whole series of images, scenes, happenings, flashed through my mind. How extraordinary memory is, and how strangely it sometimes works. Events, moments, which had remained dormant for decades were suddenly brought back.

Including one episode I had completely forgotten. Not true. Repressed, would be a much more appropriate way of expressing this.

John had a sister, Celia, some four years older. When visiting John at home, I had seen her from time to time. I doubt if she even noticed me. The age difference, at that time of life, could have been light years. Even as a girl she was beautiful, always seemed serene and self-confident. She had no lack of admirers, and for a time went out with the head-boy at my school who himself was very good-looking, self-confident, appeared to have the world at his feet as he was successful at seemingly everything. They were an impressive couple. This I registered at a distance. However, as with so many early friendships, this one must have come to an end.

As I have already mentioned, after leaving school I moved away from this part of the country. However from conversations with John I learned that Celia was working in London. Before one of my occasional visits to the city I happened to tell John of my plans, who unexpectedly suggested I contact Celia. This seemed a slightly strange idea because, as already indicated, I hardly knew her. Initially I dismissed the thought, but on one of my days in London I had a free evening. I decided I would try to contact her. I reached her on my first attempt and was surprised at how friendly, indeed even keen she seemed for us to meet. She was free that evening.

When we met, I remained in a state of never-ending surprise for the whole of the evening. Instead of finding myself on edge, nervous that she would find me somehow lacking, immature – which, on reflection, I clearly was – here was this very attractive young woman treating me as an equal and taking genuine interest in everything about me. I have rarely felt so at ease in all my life.

After such a very long time I now haven't the faintest idea what we talked about, or indeed who did the talking. It was nevertheless one of those rare occasions when two people feel comfortable in each other's company. We were both completely relaxed. Almost as if we were old friends, which of course we were not.

At the end of the evening we both went our separate ways. I was staying with an elderly aunt. Unfortunately, when I reached her flat, nobody answered the bell. She must have gone to bed. She had not wanted to give me a key.

Perhaps she was apprehensive that it would get lost, or stolen. That however was not my immediate problem.

I was not earning very much at the time and somehow didn't fancy trying to find a hotel. I phoned Celia, fortunately without having to wake her. She could not have been more understanding and suggested that I come over immediately. She, like so many young people in London then, as now, shared accommodation. Her two flatmates were away. She didn't seem at all surprised – or suspicious – at what I told her had happened. She made us coffee, even found some pyjamas her brother had left behind on one of his visits. We continued chatting, before I left her to go to my room.

After undressing, I clambered into bed, and had just opened a book from the bedside table when there was a knock on the door. Celia came in, and sat on the bed. As if she was, or seemed, eager to continue our conversation which, for a while, we did. I remained where I was, half-sitting against the pillows. Conversation slowly, finally, petered out. Celia looked at me. I suppose I must have looked at her. She breathed in sharply, looked at me again. And then, as if having made a decision, leant forward and kissed me on the cheek. As my mother might have done. She got up, said goodnight quietly, and left.

But of course she wasn't my mother. Perhaps she had seen into my unknowing mind. I shall never know.

Celia was just as friendly, indeed seemed quite unchanged, when I left the next morning. But for some strange, inexplicable reason, I never got in touch again.

I remained where I was, sitting at the table, thinking back, looking unseeingly at the local paper which had sparked off such a string of memories. Such a string of totally unconnected memories.

The Beginning of an End

All at once everything had become clear. There was no way forward, no way back. Indeed no way at all.

The matter had been going on for such a long time. Five long years. Years of hopes which had sometimes risen but which had mostly been dashed. Of late increasingly.

Earlier, initially, there had been a sense of something which had drawn them together, which had been the spark. An occasional sign. Even an occasional, of late increasingly rare embrace. Always, almost immediately, a withdrawal. An inability to commit, or take a further step. In spite of instinctive seemingly common awareness of feelings shared.

He had, up to this moment, always believed there would be a point at which a threshold would be crossed, although he was equally aware of what that threshold implied. But now he had crossed a different threshold.

He had quietly and carefully made preparations. There was a sense of urgency, but no hurry. Suddenly there was no longer any threat. If anything a curious sense of imminent relief.

And then he had phoned. One last time. Not, by what he said, to intimate what he intended to do. Quite out of the blue she had said something utterly unexpected. Also quite unprovoked on his part. For some strange reason he could not remember precisely what she had said. Her words had nevertheless conveyed to him that although she was happy to have him around he was, in essence, just a feature in her life. Perhaps it was that casual word. Implying that whether he was there or not was, ultimately, of no great significance to her, in any meaningful way.

He was thinking of this as he took out the length of tubing which he had prepared, and slowly cut it into smaller pieces before dropping these into the bin. As he turned to go back into the house he suddenly noticed his wife coming down the road towards him.

Lines of Communication

"You remind me of someone I once knew," she said.

"Oh," I replied, looking up, "it happens quite often."

This was true. I seem to have a face which provokes recognition. I don't know why this should be but it is something with which I have to live. As if my face, when viewed by others, suddenly adapts to whatever features they are recollecting.

It was also a classic situation. Two complete strangers finding themselves caught up in that curious intimacy created by being together in a railway carriage. Not that I had been the one to start talking. Quite the reverse.

I had gone down the train and had been relieved to find a compartment that was empty. I had settled comfortably into my seat, and had just opened a newspaper when my peace was shattered. An elderly woman, whose mouth was already open as she entered. Indeed she was already in mid-sentence. What followed was addressed at me.

The flow of words continued, although not once

did she again look directly at me. Then she stopped, and did look.

"Yes," she continued, "but you're much fatter."

Another curious phenomenon. The way people – once they think they have detected similarities with someone they have known – will talk as if I am not present. Since this is a situation which happens from time to time I was not as perturbed as I otherwise might have been at being described in such unflattering terms.

"My goodness," she went on, "how your face takes me back."

I found myself unable to respond to this strange statement and remained silent while she continued her lengthy study of my face. Again I wasn't even unduly upset, as I realised that what she was doing was not in fact looking at my face – although she was of course doing that – but was attempting to bring back those features which the initial glance at me had caused her to recall.

"D'you know, I think I'd probably have married him. If he'd proposed. The fool!"

"Fool?"
"Yes, fool. Did he think I was going to wait for ever. Or even worse, ask him myself?"

"I believe it is sometimes done today. Perhaps he was shy."
"Today?" she snapped. "We're talking about nearly fifty years ago."

I suddenly found myself looking at her hands. She caught my glance.

"Oh yes. I did marry."
"But not that young man?"
"Harry? No, I didn't marry Harry. My goodness, that sounds funny."
She laughed. "No, in fact I married twice. The first was hopeless."

"But this young man. . ."

"Well, even you must have been young once."
"That is true. It was also a very long time ago. But my young days could hardly be taken as a universal model. Everyone is different. And I imagine that at some stage you must have liked him. What's more, you said that you had even thought of him as a prospective husband."

"Oh, I liked him all right. It was impossible not to like him. That was partly the problem. He was so damned nice." She paused.

"In what way?"

"It's so difficult to explain. After all this time." She looked up.

"He had your eyes." she said suddenly. "That's what it is."

"You said he was 'nice'."

"He was so different from the others. They were all so pleased with themselves, totally self-centred. Or hopeless!"

"You seem to like that word. But Harry . . ." I persisted, at the same time taking myself back. I did not wish her to read too much in my face.

For a moment she was silent, obviously thinking back. Shades of youth. She was not even looking at me any more. The lines in her face softened, her eyes brightened, clearly concentrating on something in the distant past.

"Yes, Harry. How he could dance. Wonderful. Wonderful! Do you?" she asked suddenly, her tone hardening.

"Do I look as if I did?"

"No. Actually you don't." Her gaze returned to my person, travelling down slowly from head to toe. Even though I have become used to such intense scrutiny there are moments when I find being regarded as one might a piece of meat on a slab distinctly unnerving.

"I mean there was a time," I added imprudently. Fortunately she wasn't listening. In fact I had the distinct impression that she only listened when she wanted to. This reminded me vaguely of someone I had once known. A passing thought. I dismissed it.

"You're married of course!"

Not so much a question, more a confirmation. Now it was my turn to look at her. More closely. Even if I have become accustomed to having my face used for the most random comparisons, I was slowly beginning to find this form of personal interrogation a little trying. I inclined my head slightly. It wasn't exactly a nod but nor was it a clear denial. It seemed appropriate in the circumstances.

"I thought so. You have that sort of look. Children?"

This time I shook my head distinctly, which silenced her. Briefly.

"That reminds me. Harry did actually talk about

having children. I think he liked them. But that's not the same as proposing, is it?

"No." I replied.

"Isn't it strange how things will come back to haunt one after such a huge number of years?"

"Haunt?"

"Well perhaps I should have said 'remind'." She almost smiled. Again an awareness of something sensed. What was it about that half smile?

"Why are you looking at me like that?" Her tone had sharpened again.

"I was thinking," I managed to say. "I'm sorry."

"I should think so" she went on. "It's not very nice being looked at like that. By a complete stranger."

"I couldn't agree more", I hastened to add, registering that the irony of what she was saying completely escaped her. She was clearly someone who lived totally in the closed world of her own perceptions. Again that sense that I was missing something important, something which was trying to reveal itself.

She in turn had directed her attention once more at me, and was staring fixedly. I realised that something would have to be done. That there were things I did not wish her to discover from any further study of my features. In so far as it is possible I concentrated on removing any visible form of emotion from my face. This may sound strange, but I had a very strong feeling that this was something which needed to be done to prevent any further information being dragged from my unwilling person.

"He's dead," she said. Another of those extraordinary statements she seemed to produce from time to time.

"I beg your pardon. Who is?" I asked.

"My husband. I've just been trying to sort out . . . problems. I moved away." She lifted her head in that curious jerky way she had of doing anything. I looked at the bag beside her. There was a luggage label attached, name and address in large capital letters. I suddenly went very very cold. I was deeply startled, though not for the fraction of a second did I permit my state of shock to show. The woman's first name was Wendy. That was enough.

And I remembered. Suddenly, after all those years. She was the only person who had ever called me Harry. It had always irked, although when one is in love such things do no more than unconsciously irritate.

And I had been in love – with this woman who was now sitting directly opposite me. Yet fifty years later I had been unable to recognise her. All that my appearance had done for her was to awaken memories. Memories of unhappiness. Brief unhappiness. I know that because I heard of her marriage some months after my departure. I will now never know how unhappy she had been. I certainly wasn't going to ask.

I had not, I have to admit this, behaved well. Everyone had expected us to marry. I had, as I have indicated, been in love. Whatever that might mean. Somehow, although opportunities had presented themselves, sometimes I feel sure instigated, prompted by Wendy herself, I had never been able to say the words. Relations had cooled, though I always had the impression that I could have returned. I didn't. I went away. It was not an episode of which I was proud. And now, so many years later, I was sitting opposite a woman I might have married. I was retreating further and further into myself.

Under no circumstances was Wendy now to discover that the person she had been talking to was the man she had intended to marry.

We quite clearly had nothing more to say to each other. Even our memories, after such a passage of years, were different. Wendy had lost a husband. It was clearly my duty to ensure that she retained in her recollections the Harry she had known as a young man, and not the unrecognisable elderly person to whom she had been talking. That at least I still owed her.

But how was I to maintain this fragile facade for the rest of the journey. I need not have worried. At the next station another woman came into our compartment. Wendy turned to her immediately, never stopped talking to her, so that I was permitted to preserve my anonymity until we both reached our different destinations.

A Morning in Northern Ireland

When he took the shotgun out of the case he immediately noticed that the barrels needed oiling. Automatically he first reached for the ramrod, afterwards wiping an oily rag along the blue-black metal before slipping the gun back into its case. He put it away, beside his own.

He sat down, coughed, pulled out cigarette paper and began to roll tobacco. Having lit up, he settled back in his chair and looked out unseeingly across the waters of the lough.

"We know where your son is," they had said. He could still hear the rattle of boots on the gravel as they moved off. They had not come back. He would have been ready the next time. They knew that. His ears would have registered the telltale sounds.

The dog at his feet stared up at him, eyes full of interest, as if waiting for something to happen.

The big man heaved himself up, straightened, and went towards the door, motioning to the dog that there was to be no noise. As they went along the hallway he slowed briefly as he passed the door behind which his wife would be sitting.

From the rack beside the front door he lifted the

rod, already made up. Outside, a chill wind ruffled his thinning hair before he pulled on a cap. The big black dog padded beside him as they went down towards the lough, occasionally looking up to the man. The dog stopped when a bird rose out of the grass. The man moved on, making no sign.

They came to the shore. There were two boats, one roped to a ring attached to the boards of the jetty, the other just showing above the surface. There was an area of calm water between the two sides just showing. The man did not even glance at the sunken boat. The dog jumped into the boat beside the jetty while the man untied the rope, got in, before automatically loosening the petrol cap. There was a slight hiss of released air. The man turned, took on board the rod and fishing bags. With an oar he pushed the boat out before starting the motor.

The boat cut cleanly through the surface ripple, waves spreading behind as the boat picked up speed. The man sat in the stern, his attention concentrated on what lay ahead, no longer even registering the rush of cold air against his face.

He was thinking of the boy. They had gone out like this so many times. The father calm, the boy eager to be out there. The dog stood, with two feet resting on the bow planking, always eager to see what lay ahead.

Within a short time they reached the island. There was a line of calm water where the ripples ended in the shelter of the trees. The man switched off the engine, let the boat slide forward as it slowed and slowed. His attention was fixed on the water ahead. Nothing seemed to be moving. Perhaps it was too early. He had plenty of time. Automatically he reached into his pocket for a cigarette, lit it without taking his eyes off the water. It had suddenly gone very quiet. The wind seemed to be dying away, as it sometimes will.

The sun showed briefly. The man looked up. From where he was he could see the church on the hill. The stone, white, was clearly visible, glinting then fading as clouds caused the light of the sun to go away.

What had the papers said: ". . .much loved by both communities . . . a sense of shock . . . of loss . . . a policeman committed to the pursuit of justice." It was known who had committed this act. No witnesses had come forward.

It was even said that the killer had passed in front of the church on the day of the funeral.

The man thought briefly back to his wife sitting,

as she so often did, alone in that room behind a closed door. He shut his eyes for a moment.

He sensed something, looked up automatically. A ring showed in the surface, widened. The man remained motionless. Perhaps something was about to happen. But he had time. So much time. In fact he had all the time in the world.

Irish Postman

Hello, God bless, it's only me. . . . You're new here, aren't you? Yes, I thought so. . . . A lovely old house, isn't it? I've known all the people who lived here. Yes, all the people. What? Oh, . . . thank you. A cup of tea would be grand. It's dry work, walking. And I've a couple of letters somewhere. I'll give them to you. Yes, a grand house. I've known all the people . . . Very sad about the last. But then we all have to go, don't we? Not you, of course, you're young. At least not yet. I mean, not for an eternity. . . . What. . . me? Ah, bless you, all me life. I've lived all me life in these parts. And I've known people. I've known all the people here. You do . . . round here. It's not like the city. Yes, lovely. Lovely area. Not a lovelier. And I've been all over. All over here, that is. Ah, but seeing new people takes me back. And I know this house. Like the back of my hand. Anything wrong, you just ask. You just . . . ask . . . me. Post and odd jobs, that's me. In a nutshell, so to speak, Yes . . . yes . . . yes. It takes me back. I've been in and out this house since I was no bigger than a blade. A blade of grass. And as thin. What? Oh yes, I keep fit. I look after myself. Not like some of them youngsters. Ah, bless you, I keep fit. It's work and keeping busy does it. Never a dull moment. Never . . . a . . . dull moment. I can tell you. That's what's kept me young. Ah, but it's not what it was. Time was when you'd only meet open doors. Only . . . open doors. Now there's thieving. Even here. Even in this lovely part, there's thieving. Comes from the cities. And all this . . . this transportising. People can't stay still any more. They move. They move all the time. They never stop. I've lived by myself, so I know. Well, in recent years. No. . . no. . . no. Never married. I was with me father, till he died. God bless him. Grand old man. Well into his eighties he was. Fit . . . as a fiddle. Fit . . . as . . a fiddle. No, no, I've got me dogs. They keep you on your feet. A dog's grand company. The greatest. Really, the greatest. I shoot over them. I've trained dogs. The greatest, really, the greatest. With a friend. Ah, he's no more. But he was a friend. What a friend. And he could tell stories. The stories he could tell. I wish I could tell them like he could. The crack. Ah, the crack. I broke my sides when he told a story. But he's no more. So many are no more. He went last year. My best friend. It was sad. Struck him down it did. Suddenly. Within three months he was gone. Dead and gone. And . . . do you know . . . I couldn't visit him. Another friend told me not to. He was proud. . . the one that was ill. He couldn't bear to be seen in the state he was in. Wasn't that strange. I tell you, that was strange. And mighty sad. When I think of the crack. You'd have burst your sides listening to him. And dead in three months.

How life is. How . . . life . . . is. But I've lived a life. What a life I've had. The sights I've seen. And they say you don't . . . living in the country. But they don't know. They just don't know . . . do they?

Achilles Heel

It was one of those days. We had been out all morning and the rain had never stopped, or eased. We were both a little under the weather. One of those times when you wonder why you do it. I said as much to Tom, who just laughed.

"Well you keep coming back," he said.
"What about lunch?" I replied.
"May as well. The fish don't seem to like the rain either."

He brought us to the shore, clambered into the water and pulled the boat up over the rocks. He waited to help me.

"Careful now! It's slippery."
"Thank you, I'm not as steady on my feet as I once was."
"Ah, you do pretty well, and you've been at it longer than most."

Tom took out the bags, went up to the hut on the island where we generally stop in the middle of the day. He had a fire going in minutes. We took off wet coats and sat in the hut, waiting for the warmth to get through.

"Why do we do it?" I repeated. "More to the point, why do you do it? And you live here!"

"That's why," Tom said. "That's why I'm here," he continued, nodding in the direction of the lough.

"But you're not local."

I looked at him. He was so young, or seemed young to me. Yet I knew he was already in his late thirties. A powerful figure, he looked even bulkier in the clothes he was wearing. I always felt comfortable when out with him. He was never flustered, as if nothing could take him by surprise. A great comfort on lakes where conditions can change suddenly.

"No, but I've been living here for as long as you've been coming." That was very true. He had offered to take me out on my first visit, and we had continued fishing together ever since.

"There's nothing quite like these big loughs," he went on, "they're wild, really wild. They don't give in easily. You have to live with them, study them constantly, always have them in mind. In all their strangeness. That's the challenge."
"But you can't fish all the time."
"I don't."
"And?"
"Well, I can still be thinking. I follow the moods of the lake, like you would with a person."
"Identification?"

"Ah, it's not easy finding words. I mean it's different when I'm out with other people. Then I have to think of them – and *for* them often enough."
"I should hope so."
"Oh, I didn't mean you. We're friends. I can relax with a friend."

I had never really thought about our relationship. At least not like that. Two weeks a year is not a long time. Yet very intense. Day after day, sharing a boat, with everything that can happen in boats. Whims of weather. Catching fish. Or not catching fish. Being in a favourable spot. Being out when things are happening. On big lakes little can be taken for granted which, I suppose, is part of the fascination.

"It's different when I'm by myself."
"Oh, why?"
"Because I'm by myself. There's just me, the elements, and what I'm after."
"But you come from the city."
"That's just it. I couldn't stand being in cities any more. It all got on top of me. I had to get away."
"But from what you've told me, you were not alone."
"You mean my girlfriend?"
"Of course."

He paused. "I suppose she will never understand."
"Did you ever discuss the matter?"
"It was pretty hopeless. She never liked me fishing anyway."
"Her rival."
"I suppose you could put it like that."
"Actually, worse than a rival."
"What do you mean?"
"She might have won . . . against another woman."
"You could be right there," he murmured expressionlessly, continuing to stare out into the lake. "But what about yourself? You keep coming."
"That's different."
"Why is it so different. You once told me it was to get away."
"At the beginning, it was."
"You had a wife."
"You know that."
"Yes, but you left her."
"Yes, eventually I left her."
"Ever regret it?"
"No."
"Well, there you are."
"Ah, but with me it was different."
"As you said. But why?"
"I was unhappy. Desperately unhappy. Were you?"
"I begin to see what you're getting at. No. . . I

wasn't unhappy. . ."
"But?"
"I had this yearning. To be alone. Untied. So I could live this through."
"This?"

I looked at him. The same indefinable something in his expression. I thought back to what I knew of him. In essence not very much. Small surface details. Like his work, for example. He restored furniture, antique furniture. I had never actually seen him at his work – I don't think he would have welcomed that – but I had seen the results. In his workshop. It was amazing that such huge hands could perform such delicate operations. He had to show me precisely what it was that had been restored, because his work was executed so perfectly. Perfection. A difficult word, since perfection implies a total exclusion, permitting, or allowing for no weakness. Perhaps "beauty" would be more appropriate, because beauty is visible, can be felt, is almost indefinable.

"Now don't get me wrong. I like my work. Restoring gives me huge satisfaction. It means I can be my own boss. I'm totally independent. And there are big challenges to face in what I do. Very often you have to puzzle and puzzle before you find the right way of making any given piece of furniture, after treatment, look as it should. Genuine. And I genuinely enjoy that. But it is nevertheless a limited satisfaction. At least for me.

Whereas out on the lake, however much you think you know, you never stop suddenly facing situations in which whatever you thought you knew doesn't work, situations which will defeat you. And that's a very different challenge . . . one which never ends."

"But fish, even big fish, have brains the size of a pea."
"I knew you would say something like that. Can you not be serious?"
"Perhaps I was being serious."

And who knows, perhaps I was being serious. Perhaps I was also putting the question to myself! Perhaps I was approaching a sense of personal inadequacy, because Tom was so good at everything he did. For example, being out in a boat with him meant accepting his superiority. Anything I achieved was achieved largely because of what he made possible. And everything he did was somehow just right. If he was casting a fly, for instance, every movement seemed calculated – no, not calculated – was naturally synchronised to achieve the greatest effect with a minimum of physical effort. I could only watch in admiration, without ever having the slightest suspicion that what he did was done to impress. He was always too much absorbed in what he was doing to leave any room for personal vanity.

"So this activity . . . this obsession . . . has in fact given you what you felt you were missing out on. In your earlier life?"

"I have never really attempted to define what it is finally. . . ultimately."

"Could you?"

"I'm not sure. I imagine – now that you put it to me – it has to be that what I experience out here on the lake is a feeling that you never reach the end, that essentially you never get beyond the beginning. With the road stretching out there ahead of you."

"And that makes you happy."
"That's a big word."
"You haven't answered my question."
"Can one?"
"You could try. For example, your private life. What about . . . personal relations."
"That too is not an easy question."
"Well, there must be women around. Even here."
"Of course there are."

"And?"

"They seem to have different expectations. I mean I'm not talking about casual encounters. And of course most in my age group are already married, or have moved away."

"And the younger ones?"

"They have a different . . . agenda. I suppose I must seem old. To them."

"And your old girlfriend?"

"She would never live here."

"But you have established something. You have an aim, a challenge that will – to use your words – never go away. ."

"Do you know something," Tom suddenly said, "I think the rain is easing. There's even a bit of light in that sky. I think we should be getting back on to the lough. We've a lot to catch up on."

A Deeply Objective Fairy Tale

Once upon a time – say, until about twenty years ago – there was a beautiful river which meandered through beautiful unspoiled countryside. The water, which flowed down from a huge reservoir, was crystal clear and cold; so cold, a perfect habitat for the many kinds of fish which thrived in this unspoiled stream. Sadly there were also men. Humans. Mostly from the city. They wished to share in this paradise. So all along the banks of this beautiful river they reserved sections where they could stay. With their caravans, their tents, their dogs, their children, and their disturbance of erstwhile peace.

The children and adults played and swam in the river, throwing stones, making noise where there had previously been nothing but the sound of birds and water. The dogs barked, chased animals and birds, also fouling the banks with what dogs do.

Then something happened to the water. It was no longer quite so clear, quite so pure. Men had again interfered, by introducing invisible but poisonous substances, because local politicians did not wish to spend money on filtering effluent before it entered the river. Soon, at certain times of the year, the river bed became covered in thick brown slime. Plants could not grow, insects suffocated, the sun's rays could not penetrate this brown sludge and the river began to die.

Then more city ideas were put into practice, because people are so much more important than nature. Nature has no genuine lobby. Nature just suffers and dies. Slowly. Or fast. Nature does not know the word compromise. Pathways were created along both banks, so that cyclists in droves could speed through what had been a bird sanctuary.

Later city-dwellers started coming in ever greater numbers, with their canoes and paddle-boats. Not only disturbing the river, but also tearing out plants on their way down the river.

There had always been anglers, who came, made no noise, fished occasionally, but who kept a watchful eye on the river. They struggled to look after the river and its rightful occupants.

And then, largely because of laws made by men who foolishly believe that nature today will still find its own balance, cormorants – birds which have no natural enemies – were declared a protected species; so that on this river where there had been none, suddenly there were, at certain seasons, hundreds. The river is now almost totally devoid of fish.

With the result that what was once upon a time, now really *is* once upon a time. This river which was formerly so beautiful, so pure, so unspoiled, is now just one more playground for human beings who want to play but not pay. Or think. Or preserve. Or think any further than the weekend ahead. And that is the end of this deeply objective fairy tale.

Secret Sharer

When you have lived in a place for a period of time things tend to fall into a pattern, particularly if most days are spent working at home. So much so that inevitably each day becomes a space of time in which certain things recur at certain very specific moments. That is how it should be. It makes for continuity and brings its own reward.

Only the other day I found myself looking out of the window shortly after nine in the morning. Expectantly. Nothing happened. Because this had become part of a regular but totally unconscious habit, I was suddenly very aware. Aware that something should have, but hadn't happened. For a moment I was unable to think what it was.

And then he appeared.

That was when I realised what had been missing. An unmistakable figure. Quite unmistakable. The figure of a man bent forward, face only half visible beneath a large-brimmed hat pulled down, a man striding purposefully, grimly forward. He passed this way, every day, at almost exactly the same time. There was a rhythm, an unmistakable rhythm, in that stride. A kind of flexible inflexibility. Almost as if this man was being moved by some outside agency.

The figure passed, and I could sink back into whatever it was that I would then normally and regularly do. But of course it was not quite the same, because the man had been slightly later than usual. I realised that I had unconsciously been waiting for him to pass.

I had never spoken to this man. Not only because I was never out of my room at that time. We occasionally passed each other in the street at other times of the day.

He never spoke.

That is not quite correct. Sometimes he did speak. To himself. On occasions he would be addressing others. Not visible others. Just others, who must have been somewhere within the range of his voice.

I was sometimes able to make out individual words, single phrases, which somehow did not make the man, or what he was expressing, any more understandable. Yet he always seemed full of purpose.

But what was it about this man? Strange as it may sound, he struck me almost as a figment of his own imagination. Almost as if he had been created specially. There was something very unusual, almost inhuman about him. And yet he was human. Perhaps it is because most people, even if they have been formed by life, still somehow convey an impression of fallibility. Curious word. I wonder why such a word should suddenly come to mind. Perhaps again it was that unrelenting purposefulness of his movements. And of course his appearance which, while part and all of him, was somehow . . . imposed. Whether from inside or outside I shall never know because, as I have already said, we never spoke.

Again I find myself pausing, because while that is also true it is not quite correct. Sometimes on passing him in the street I had the impression that he had something to communicate. He would give me a look, the like of which I have never experienced in any other person. He looked straight at and into me, touching some distant chord. He appeared to be attempting to say something, a form of communication for which the eyes are not designed. It is said that the eyes are the mirror of the soul. Even if that should be true, this was a soul whose depths I would not wish to enter. I tended to look away, or break eye contact, as far as this was possible. Although his eyes had a strangely compelling force which almost prevented contact from being broken. And in spite of the fact that the look came darkly from under that wide-brimmed hat.

Ah, the hat. All at once I again find myself reflecting. On the hat. What was it about that hat which had so caught my attention? Why should a perfectly ordinary hat be any cause for reflection? After all there is nothing at all unusual in choosing to wear a hat – even if always the same hat – at precisely the same angle.

Yet it wasn't only the hat.

It had something to do with the whole appearance of the man. That hat, to mix a metaphor, started to ring bells, bells which continued to ring, if faintly, at the back of my mind.

Having always lived away from people – my work makes this imperative – I have rather let the world pass me by. I am reflective by nature. Ephemeralities, everyday happenings, hardly touch me. Even if, as in the case of this strange man, they can sometimes involuntarily impose themselves, can even become a part – whether desired or desirable – of daily routine.

Nevertheless, as the appearance of this man

proves, it is not possible always to withdraw totally from what is going on all around one. Certain things, sounds, images, will somehow still manage to enter one's own personal space.

The hat.

What was it about that confounded hat? This object, this . . . image, nagged. I couldn't place it. Which was doubly irritating, as I prefer to have order in my life. I do not like . . . not knowing. Which is another reason for keeping people, other people that is, at a distance. Away, apart from me. People can be, nearly always are, unpredictable, which again is not good. For me. How can I possibly concentrate on what I must do if other people's concerns keep entering my space and constantly interfere with what I am doing. Such things get in the way. In the way of what I am doing. Something which I do not like. At all.

Now don't get me wrong. I have nothing actually against other people. It's just that I don't need them. So often they will want to get into one's life. In my case, there's no need. It's strange. One can make this so clear, but others sometimes, often, just don't want to accept this. They intimate that one is missing something if one keeps to oneself. Personally I have the impression that I would be losing something if I constantly had to mix with others.

Whatever is essential, intrinsic, worth holding on to, somehow gets lost in the complexities of other people's lives. What's more, and worse, such social obligations would get in the way of my work.

It is essential for me to have fixed times. Otherwise I fall behind with what concerns me most. Something I find intolerable.

Which brings me back to the man with the hat who passes my house at precisely the same time every day. He has – or had – become almost an essential part of my daily routine. In a way, I suppose, his appearance gave me an unconscious indication that I must start. So that, without in any way interfering, he had become an unwitting spur at the beginning of each day's activity.

And then, suddenly, he was late, and that pushed him forward in my mind and, as a consequence, caused something to get between me and what I should have been doing. So that now, instead of being able to concentrate, I was being distracted. And above all, by that hat.

This so affected me that totally against all my normal practice I opened the window. I generally keep the windows shut because otherwise noise – birds, cars, people – becomes audible, which again of course causes something to get between me and what I am doing. On this occasion this is exactly what happened, although I had already given up any hopes of just picking up from where I had left off. Just as I opened the window, a car passed, one of those new vehicles, roof down, driven by some thoughtless young philistine, radio on, sounds blasting off into the surrounding neighbourhood. The noise! At first it was just the noise which grated on my nerves. But then as the sounds entered my consciousness, they took on a more recognisable form. A tune from a song which had been popular years and years and years ago. Normally I wouldn't even have registered anything at all. I live so much a life of the mind. But there was a time when I would occasionally listen to the radio.

A theme, a few bars from this piece had somehow stayed with me. I couldn't name the singer, because popular singers have never interested me. Nevertheless my memory was jogged. And suddenly I remembered. It was like an electric shock. A photograph, reproduced everywhere. Like a trademark. A photograph of that singer.

And that was the moment when I identified the hat. The hat on the strange man.

He was dressed exactly like that singer all those years ago.

So I had been right in my surmises all along. That this man somehow had no genuine personal identity but that he had created himself in the image of somebody else. This gave me a huge sense of relief. Not because this man had affected me in any way. Nor because I in any way identified myself with him. No, it was because I had been proved right in my assumption.

With the result that I now could put him behind me, and go forward confidently. After all, it was none of my concern what identity this man chose to adopt.

Nevertheless it does seem a little strange, when every human being has, and is, a unique personality – and I naturally include myself – that one should feel impelled to form oneself in the image of somebody else.

Very strange indeed.

Safe Distance

I was rather surprised when Regine opened the door. Even more when she came forward and shook my hand.

"This is very formal," I said, in German. "Any reason?"

"Well, yes, I may not have another chance, and I wanted to take this opportunity of saying goodbye." Regine continued, smiling very warmly at me, her eyes widening.

"Goodbye?" I replied, even more surprised. "Are you leaving?"

"No, definitely not. But I think you may be!"

"Oh," I responded, although I was now no longer quite so surprised. If anyone knew what was happening in the office, she did.

"Yes. I think you'd better go through to the boss. Immediately."

I couldn't for the life of me think what might have occurred to provoke such excitement. At the time I was working at the agency only as a part-time translator.

It was a very typical situation, one of many which can happen when English is involved. Most of the people I dealt with seemed to think they were experts which, in a way, they often were. Yet some things cannot be argued. Only a native speaker can ultimately know. At least that was how I then thought.

But in this instance it was the native speaker who had slipped up, and the mistake had caught the attention of an ambassador. Very embarrassing. Very embarrassing indeed. I stood in the office in front of the boss and straight away apologised for a most unfortunate error. The storm passed over. I was not fired.

In the event it was Regine who left, although not immediately. Not because she was dismissed but because she had found a job which would take her to Brazil.

All of this flashed through my mind again as I held in my hand the letter which I had just discovered at the back of a drawer. So many things came back.

In fact Regine was very attractive, something I noticed the first time I entered the agency. She very quickly registered the effect that her appearance had on me. I gained the impression that she was somehow interested.

It became a sort of game – at least for me – to play up to her, without ever making a move. Without ever inviting her out. Something held me back.

I glanced down at the letter, which had reached me some months after Regine had left for Brazil. It was very revealing:

". . . Trying to speak in Portuguese makes me forget a lot of my English. I beg your pardon, but on Sunday morning I took a bath in Portuguese literature and poets, and I sometimes find myself speaking English translating from Portuguese."

No, Regine was not a person who ever did things by halves. She continued:

"Right now I am seeing far on the horizon a little cloud of hope for solution of my problems. I can still imagine your very busy face, and right now, I am trying to imitate it. . ."

There I think her memory must already have been playing her false, as my face is one part of myself which I keep firmly under control. It is, I suppose, possible that the mask may on occasion have slipped.

A little later in the letter she became somewhat

more specific on the subject of her "hopes on the horizon."

". . . So I happen to have lost part of my heart again (it is strange how many times she can lose only one heart – didn't you say that!) to a Brazilian person."

Later she became even more precise:

". . . Just one more information – the gentleman (it is the other executive secretary sitting in one room with me) is the one I am trying to give my heart to. As this is always is a very difficult thing, we are thinking of planning our future together when he is back. . . . The poor fellow tried (just as you are doing) to live his life alone, and has to face serious problems right now, having changed his aims."

I was rather intrigued by the phrase: "the one I am trying to give my heart to. . ." Somehow this is just what I could imagine her doing, and probably being very successful.

In the very next paragraph Regine suddenly switched back to her time in Germany:

"I sometimes have a very sad feeling when thinking back. All the nice persons in the agency. I was sometimes trying so very hard to make you invite

me, because I really could imagine how much nonsense one can do with you."

I put the letter down, and reflected. I could suddenly once again see the warmth of the smile on Regine's face as she opened the door on the day she thought I was to be dismissed. It was a smile to remember, and one I had not forgotten. It had also made things clear. Very clear.

One or two sentences in the letter I would probably also not forget:

"We are thinking about planning our future together."

It is perhaps no bad thing if there is somebody close who is happy, willing, and determined, to help one plan the future.

A Bit on the Side

"Don't you miss the old days?"
"What old days?"
"When you were travelling."
"Not really."
"Wasn't it fun, travelling?"
"Not really."
"You surely must have something to tell. . . . To an old friend? Some dark secret!"
"Does it sound as if I had?"

We were sitting in the clubhouse after our weekly round of golf.
"But travel is supposed to broaden the mind," Peter said.
"Not the kind of travelling I used to do."
"Now you're not going to tell me that in the twenty-five years you spent on the road, nothing happened," Peter continued. "I mean, what did you do in the evenings?"
"Precious little, mostly. It's a long day when you've been driving, trying to get to appointments on time, and not falling behind some idiot's overly tight schedule."
"Never? Nothing? Come on."
"Not really."
"What's that supposed to mean?"
"Well, I did have one very odd experience. Very odd. I got picked up."
"What's so odd about that?"

"It's not the sort of thing that happens to me. I suppose I'm not the type. Never have been."

For once Peter made no comment. He just looked at me, expressionlessly.

"I'll have to think back for a moment. It's so many years ago. Somewhere in the north. Not sure I can even recall the name of the town, although I do remember the hotel. Usual pokey sort of place. For once I'd finished a bit early and was sitting in the bar having a drink. It was quite full, but not crowded. In the middle was a kind of island with a leather-covered seat all round on which people were sitting. I can't think why I should remember that. Except that it all looked very uncomfortable. Tiny windows along one wall, and just about enough light to read by. Not what I'd call cosy, but I wasn't in the mood for going out.

Most of the people there were either women who appeared to have come in from the country shopping, or men having a drink before going home. As I say, I was sitting by myself, looking at the paper, not really taking in what I was reading. It was all local stuff anyway.

I suddenly noticed a girl sitting near me. Actually that's not quite true. It was more that I became aware of something. I turned, and there was this girl tipping everything out of her handbag. Then she grabbed a comb and began putting things back into the bag again.

I returned to my newspaper. Not for long. I suddenly registered that someone was talking to me. Muttering would be a better word, because I had difficulty understanding what she was saying.

'It's my hair,' she said.
'I beg your pardon,' I said, not catching on.
'My hair, just had it cut.' she explained. I noticed that the nails on the hand holding the comb were painted a curious shade of green.

'It's all tangled.' She held up a small mirror and tugged the comb through her hair. Or tried to.
'Look at my hands!' she continued, holding them out for my inspection. 'What do you think I've been doing all day?'

I looked. Her hands were very pale, though somehow not very clean. They had a curiously used look.
'I haven't the faintest idea,' I replied.
'Cars! Been washing cars. Bet that surprises you. Been at it all day. I can do repairs, too, but the men won't let me. Too bloody jealous.'
'Been at it long?'
'About a fortnight. Packed up today. Got something better for the end of next week. I got

fed up . . . had enough . . . Dirty buggers.' she added, in an undertone.

'Don't get me wrong,' she went on, 'I'm careful with my words. I surprised them. They never suspected I'd be like that. I can stand up for myself.'

She had a strange way of expressing herself. She kept changing, like a parrot adopting other voices. She certainly wasn't stupid. I noticed her looking at my glass.

'Can I get you a drink?' I said.

'Thanks. Vodka and orange, please.'

I went to the bar, brought back drinks for us both.

'Oh, that bitch,' she exclaimed, she's deliberately given you a large bottle of orange.'

'It doesn't matter," I said.

'I'll get it changed. Don't like wasting good money.'

And before I could stop her, she rushed off. I could sense disapproval all round me. Back she came, triumphant. Sue, she said her name was.

'Would it surprise you if I told you I'd done a job?'

'You seem to be full of surprises.'

'There were three of us. All girls. Broke into a house.

I stayed outside. On lookout. Someone must have tipped the fuzz. I only did it for kicks, bit of a dare. But they shopped us, and that was that. Suspended sentence. It wasn't easy getting a job after that. But I may have something at the end of next week.'

I didn't know whether she was having me on or not. I suppose it doesn't really matter. Probably she just wanted to provoke. Perhaps she didn't. I don't know. In the meantime she'd untangled her hair, and seemed quite pleased with what she'd done to her face. Not a bad face, actually. She insisted on buying me a drink. Then she started looking round, constantly seemed to be on the point of saying something, and became increasingly restive.

'You staying here?', she asked suddenly, jerking her head.
'Yes,' I said.
'Oh,' she reflected for a moment, "Well, I think I'd better be going.'
I said nothing.
'Tell you what,' she continued, 'how about having a drink later this evening. Somewhere else. I know a good place near where I live."
I still don't know why I didn't back out at this point. But I didn't.
'All right,' I replied, 'Can I pick you up in the car?'
'No, no,' she responded quickly, 'Let's meet there. I can tell you how to get there.
'Well, you'll have to. I don't know my way round here.'

She explained, and then left me in the now emptying room.
Well, I found the other place without much difficulty. In fact I was too early. I decided to wait in the car just in case she didn't turn up.
It would not have surprised me. But she came, only about ten minutes later than arranged.
'Nice car,' she said, adding, 'could do with a clean.'
'Be my guest.' I replied.

She grinned. The pub was still empty, except for the landlord who was washing glasses. Oldish chap, with plenty of beer round the middle. He looked at me, and then at Sue. He didn't seem overjoyed at what he saw. It was a bare, unwelcoming sort of room. High-backed wooden benches, tables, a lot of space in the middle. I brought over drinks. We sat, not speaking, not even looking at each other. Sue jumped up – she was a great one for jumping up – asked me if I liked music. Without waiting for an answer she went over to the jukebox, put in money, studied the titles, pushed several knobs. When the music started – this didn't please the landlord either – she remained where she was, jigging to the rhythm. I suddenly realised how tiny, almost fragile the girl was. She turned, came over.

'Shall we dance?' she said, in one of her voices.

'It's all right. I wasn't being serious.'
'Never know with you,' I said.
'And that's just how I like it,' she replied.

The door opened. Another couple came in, both about thirty. I hardly noticed. At first. Sue kept staring across at the woman, seemed puzzled. After some minutes of this, she suddenly got up and went over to them. Or rather, to the woman. I waited, wondering. Sue put out a finger.

'I know you,' she said, 'Your hair's different.' She looked round triumphantly. The expression on the woman's face changed, eased. She recognised Sue and became quite animated. The woman chatted away. The man did not join in. He sat motionless, occasionally glancing at the girl, once briefly at me. I didn't go over. I don't know what I'd have said if I had. I remained where I was, looking across at Sue's back. It was seldom still. She seemed to need the whole of her body for complete self-expression. I couldn't hear the words because of the noise of the music.

'I knew I knew that woman,' Sue announced when she returned. She then gave me a long story about how they had met. I have forgotten the details. It was not important. She remained standing.
'Look, I just got to make a phone-call. Be back in a sec.'

She was gone. Again not for long.
'Got any change?' she asked. I gave her some coins. I was left on my own for about twenty minutes. In fact I had begun to wonder if she'd come back at all. The couple opposite took a long time over their drinks, hardly spoke, mostly looked across the room, in my direction. Our eyes never actually met.

'It was my friend. I had to get him. You don't mind?'
Three sentences rattled off in her usual breathless manner.
'You're a good sort,' she went on, not waiting for an answer. 'Most of the blokes round here would've kicked hell out of me if I'd left them like that. By the way, you weren't upset, were you?'
'What do you mean?'
'Me chatting you up like that.'
'No. Why?'
'I dunno. You looked a bit lonely.'
'I'm often by myself. . . . I travel.'
'Great. . . I bet you think I'm looking for a good time.'
'Why not. You're only young once.'
'Young!' she gave a strange laugh, 'Let me get you a drink for a change.'
'You already have,' I replied.
She got up, started to fumble in her purse.
'Oh!' she exclaimed, 'I seem to have left my

money at home . . . it's on the kitchen table. I remember . . .'

'Don't worry,' I said, 'I'm on expenses.'

'That's all right then. But I *am* sorry. I'd like to have got you a drink. You're a good sort.'

'Opinions vary,' I replied.

'Now don't get me wrong. I'm not one of them that sleep around. Fact is, I have to be bloody careful. Can't take the pill. Something went wrong with my kidneys after the second child. The doctor warned me not to have any more.'

'You're married, then.'

'You could call it that. Had to. I was eighteen, pregnant. And then my fiancé got himself killed. Motorbike. We were going to be married that month.'

'What did you do?'

'I got someone. Bloke who'd been lodging with us. He knew, of course, said it didn't matter, me being pregnant. But it did.'

'Where's your husband now?'

'Christ knows.'

'Then they took the kids away,' she added.

'Who did?'

'Welfare . . . said I couldn't manage . . . no money . . . no job . . . they came once . . . just like that . . . said I'd been drinking. What was I supposed to do?'

'But can't the police help if your husband doesn't keep up with payments?'

'Jesus! What kind of a world do you live in? D'you think the police want to know if my husband pays, or doesn't pay? Anyway, they'd never catch him. He's never there. Always on the move.'

'When did you last see him?'

'Two years ago. That was one occasion the police did come. He nearly killed me. Neighbours called the police. I was black and blue for weeks. I got out after that. Didn't want any more of that.'

'Where did you go? Back to your parents?'

'You must be joking. Only reason I wanted to marry was to get away from them. My mother died when I was thirteen. Unlucky thirteen! You can say that again. And who looked after the kids? For nothing, and nothing again! Me! Muggins. I wouldn't go back into that bastard's house if they dragged me.'

'But where do you live?'

'With my gran. She's the only one who's ever cared. She's a real pal!

The other couple got up, left without so much as a glance in our direction. Sue watched them go. She took out her purse, started to fumble in it again.

'What's the matter?' I asked.

'D'you think you could lend me a bit . . . till next week. I'm starting work again next week.'

I felt in my pockets.

'Sorry, I've only got a tenner.'
'That'd be a help.' she said, 'Thanks.'

We got up and went out together. I drove her home, to one of those endless streets of terrace houses. Two up, two down, scrubby gardens at the front. I stopped when she told me.
'Gran'll be waiting up. She always does. She'll be watching.'

I looked towards the windows of the house. Nothing moved in the weak light cast by the street lights. I could imagine the grandmother, sitting behind the curtains, peeping through.

'I'd better be going,' Sue said, 'Thanks . . . for the evening.'
'Good luck,' I replied.
'Yeah,' she answered, 'I could do with some.'
She jumped out of the car and ran up to the house, not looking round.
And that was that."

Peter was staring into his empty beer glass, running a finger round the rim. He looked up slowly when I stopped talking.
"Sounds to me as if somebody got taken for a ride," he said. "By the way, the wife asked me to check if you're both still all right for Sunday evening."
"Thanks. I'll ask Jane, and let you know. By the

way, there's no need to mention what happened, when we meet."

"Just as you like, but actually I can't for the life of me see that anything did."

"Well," I replied, "you can't say I didn't warn you."

Temps Perdu

As I came into the room I saw the chair, caught, shimmering in a shaft of sunlight. In my mind's eye that was how it had remained. Except that now, after all this time, there was no-one sitting in it.

I remained standing in the coolness of a room which had not been entered for so many years. A slight mustiness made its presence felt as I remained where I was, trying to register what was there. Even the birds seemed to have stopped singing, or perhaps no sounds penetrated from outside. I remained standing where I was. Everything was so still.

Everything? No, not everything. The echoes of voices reverberated down the corridors of my mind. I continued to stare at that chair, a mute witness to a dark distance. Distance? Yes, distance, but still and suddenly, shiningly, present. I took in the glow of the hard wood, all at once remembering that there had never been a cushion. Whoever sat on it knew how penitential that seat could be. I had never liked it.

Nor shall I ever understand why she chose to sit there at our last meeting.

Eternal Triangle

Being old – indeed very old – I have reached a point in life at which I no longer have the urge or desire to hang on. To material, or portable goods. On the contrary I am constantly on the lookout for things I do not need any more and which can be disposed of. It is a cutting-off of what lies behind – a slow elimination of the past.

For example recently, while sifting through an accumulation of papers, I pulled out an old school magazine. Before throwing it out I casually flicked through. Suddenly, at the obituary section, my attention was caught. I was surprised. Genuinely surprised. It had completely slipped my mind that what I was reading was something I had written myself. It went as follows:

Somehow it is not easy to believe that Bobbie Bishop is no longer with us. I knew Bobbie, as master and friend, for more than forty years. Early memories stay longest, shine brighter than anything which later follows. Bobbie is still fixed indelibly within that warm cocoon of childhood recollection.

He was such a nice person: a trite description, an appalling adjective. Yet, in the case of Bobbie, it somehow seems just right. He was kind, friendly, self-effacing, endlessly modest, brave, drew respect without ever seeking it, was the most patient and encouraging of teachers. A man of principle. His principles, it always seemed, were not superimposed, but an integral part of his unique personality. If there really is such a thing, he was English – in the nicest sense of the world.

I only once saw Bobbie angry: during a year in which he taught Geography – not, I imagine, one of his favourite subjects. For some reason I insisted that The Grampians (or was it the Grumpians!) were not where he said they were. Bobbie went crimson, and let me have it. I am sure he was right.

In his teaching, Bobbie made one want to go further. His love of literature was infectious, even if I have still never managed to bring myself to re-read 'Prometheus Unbound'. However I think that may be Shelley's fault. By a strange coincidence I recently came across some English essays I wrote at school. It is so revealing to read Bobbie's comments. For example: 'There is much to be said in favour of this, but the chief fault lies in a tendency to allow the general interpretation to invade the realm of the particular. I will explain the point further.' I'm sure he did. What one might call praising with very faint damns – kind, cryptic, clear.

After an interval of many decades, I have just glanced through 'Prometheus Unbound' once more. It still strikes me as excessively wordy. However I did light upon two lines which might perhaps fittingly end this piece:

'Gentleness, Virtue, Wisdom and Endurance,–
These are the seals of that most firm assurance. . .'

This short text sent my mind spinning slowly back into the past; a past detained, so to speak, at two removes. I am not only old, but have been living away from England for so long that my mental image of that country is fixed in a distant time; an image still clear, but fading.

I sat where I was with the magazine in my hands, puzzled, disturbed, by a thought I could not quite get together. Suddenly I remembered. The obituary was not as I had originally composed it. It had been savagely cut – for reasons of space, the editor had said.

Initially I had been furious. By then of course it was too late to withdraw the article. Later – much later – I had been amused. How seriously one takes oneself at certain stages of life.

If I am honest – and at my age I find it increasingly easy to be honest – I have to admit that the reasons for shortening the article could hardly have come as much of a surprise. It is after all customary to speak of the dead, in particular immediately after death, in terms of unmitigated respect. For a time at least, a veil of decency is drawn over anything which might seem negative. Not, I hasten to add, that with Bobbie there was anything negative. For me he will always remain someone in whom I could detect no blemish.

In retrospect, perhaps unconsciously, I think I must have expected what did in fact happen. The article was reduced almost by half. If I had not exactly committed a faux pas, I had nevertheless done something which was not expected. I had crossed one of those invisible lines. Thus far, and no further.

That too is one of those realisations which come late. If they come at all. Unless, that is, one is a person whose life is accompanied and directed by total consistency. How often it happens – and this is the story of my life – one is driven to do something, knowing that it will go against what is expected. Looking back, I appreciate that this is exactly what I had done.

My faux pas was to have introduced someone else into the obituary. In the person of a master who had died several years before Bobbie. Nothing wrong in that, one might think.

Unfortunately I had used this example to hold up against Bobbie. There could hardly have been a greater contrast. To start with Alex Fischer was not English. He was also, to put it mildly, very different from the other members of staff. If not a thorn in the flesh, he very definitely stood out from the rest. Again, looking back, I think it probably gave him pleasure to be different. School was a world of fixed values. For him nothing was fixed. He had fled his country. Nothing was to be fixed for him again. Ever.

In itself that was no bad thing. Eccentricity was not exactly an unusual phenomenon at the kind of school I attended. No, it was something more basic, more fundamental, which quite clearly had upset the editor of the school magazine. I had actually dared to speak badly of the dead. But, let's face it, Alex was impossible. Perhaps "thorn in the flesh" is not such an inaccurate description. Like him, hate him, it was impossible to ignore him. He lived entirely according to his own standards. That, I suppose, is also consistency of a sort. Furthermore he got results – with those pupils whom he favoured. Then the whole energy of the man was transferred to that selected boy. The results were often dramatic. Alex's pupils gained scholarships, prizes, and this reflected well on the school. Unfortunately, even Alex was human.

His attitude, his preferences, could undergo

startling changes. For example, with me. I happened to be rather good at history, and for much of one year was top of the class. Suddenly – I cannot now remember why – our relations soured. Alex actually so manipulated the marking that my ranking in class slipped. There could be no doubt, since we all kept a close watch on marks. After that, war was declared; a stormy period which lasted for at least two years.

As far as I now recollect, I used Alex in the article to demonstrate just how superior Bobbie was. Perhaps that was inappropriate. What's more one might even argue that being unfair was something I had "learned" from Alex. Alex was provocation personified.

It is interesting to note that the English word "fair" has entered the German language. It is sometimes said that if a word does not exist in a language, then what it stands for does not exist either. On the other hand, the English have taken over "Schadenfreude" from German! In any case, I am certain that for Alex "fairness" was one of those ridiculous English conventions used to make foreigners feel inferior. In fact he probably decided to act as he did both to achieve his own ends and also to prove that fairness was a bogus quality. Certainly nobody could ever accuse Alex of being fair.

Hostilities between us continued up to my last year when, to my dismay, I discovered he would be teaching me German. At the beginning of the year, to my lasting surprise, he actually suggested a truce . . . that we attempt to put up with each other. I still don't know why he did this. Certainly he rather spoiled the gesture by predicting that with all the other things I was doing I stood no chance of passing. But who knows? That remark so infuriated me that I decided to show him. I passed. Not brilliantly, but I passed.

Curiously enough, after I left school, there were only two masters with whom I continued to correspond. Bobbie and Alex. Thinking back, I assume that during this last year some kind of respect must have developed on both sides. Admittedly from two very different standpoints.

What led me however to continue keeping contact was something quite different. Relations between Bobbie and Alex had always been as stormy as between myself and Alex. For Alex, Bobbie was the perfect target for attacks on the Establishment; or what Alex considered the Establishment to be.

Nothing gave Alex greater pleasure than needling, or aggravating Bobbie. From Bobbie I would receive incandescent letters in which Alex's latest iniquities were related in every shameful detail. However I think that even Bobbie in the end came to accept Alex for what he was. Perhaps even he – Bobbie was after all the least vindictive of men – became rather amused. For quite some time their letters provided me with an endless source of entertainment.

Being a bachelor, Alex had time on his hands during school holidays, and travelled widely. Again it is curious. It was largely through an introduction of his that I finished up working abroad. Alex would visit from time to time. Completely in character, he would write short notes, indicating time of arrival and what he expected to eat. "Just a light meal" became a family phrase. He was fussy with his food, and his instructions did not go down well with my wife. However his visits were not frequent, and he was good company in the sense that being interested in all the least attractive sides of human nature he always had something of a scurrilous nature to report.

In later years his health deteriorated seriously. So much so that he was constantly holding his imminent death before us like some macabre terminal threat. It went on for a long time. With the result that when the news of his death reached my wife, she actually burst out laughing. It was just too much.

It would have been unlike Alex not to have had some trick up his sleeve, even after death. He had occasionally intimated that I featured in his will; a piece of information which, for obvious reasons, rankled.

Some months later I received a letter from a contemporary at school. After referring to Alex's death he wrote that he too had been promised "something" in the will but that in the event all had gone to a person neither of us knew!

And that really is the end of the story.

As I slowly dropped the school magazine into the waste paper basket, I couldn't help reflecting – for one last time – on those two extraordinary teachers. The one had succeeded by being a shining example; the other by provoking, and ultimately forcing one to prove him wrong.